Harriet and Walt

HARRIET AND WALT

NANCY CARLSON

Carolrhoda Books, Inc. / Minneapolis

For Gail, in memory of our winter in Norway

This book is available in two editions:
Library binding by Carolrhoda Books, Inc., a division of Lerner Publishing Group
Soft cover by First Avenue Editions, an imprint of Lerner Publishing Group
241 First Avenue North
Minneapolis, MN 55401 U.S.A.

Website address: www.carolrhodabooks.com

Library of Congress Cataloging-in-Publication Data

Carlson, Nancy L.
      Harriet and Walt / Nancy Carlson.
         p.   cm.
      Summary: During a day's playing in the snow, Harriet decides that her little brother Walt isn't as big a pest as she once thought he was.
      ISBN: 1–57505–672–0 (lib. bdg. : alk. paper)
      ISBN: 1–57505–723–9 (pbk. : alk. paper)
      [1. Dogs—Fiction. 2. Brothers and sisters—Fiction. 3. Snow—Fiction.]
   I. Title.
   PZ7.C21665Har 2004
   [E]—dc22   2003023365

Manufactured in the United States of America
1 2 3 4 5 6 – JR – 09 08 07 06 05 04

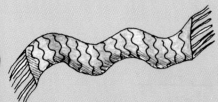

"Yippee!" yelled Harriet. "It must have snowed all night long! I'm going to play outside all day."

"Don't forget Walt," said her mother.
"Aw, Mom," said Harriet.

"Harriet," said her mother, "you take your little brother with you, and that's final."

"Oh, all right," grumbled Harriet. "Come
on, Walt."

"I'm going to make a tunnel through this snowdrift," said Harriet. "It's going to be so neat, Walt!"

And it was . . .

until Walt fell through it.
"You big dope," said Harriet.

Harriet decided to make a snow angel instead.
"Look, Walt. It's easy. You try it."

So Walt did.

"Not *that* way, Walt! Lie on your *back*," said Harriet. "Boy, oh boy, what a dummy."

"You said it!" said Harriet's friend George.
"Come on, Harriet. Let's play tag. But not
Walt. He's too little."

"Listen, Walt," said Harriet. "You stand right here by the flagpole and don't move. And whatever you do, don't put your tongue on the pole."

So Walt stood quietly by the flagpole. But pretty soon he got curious.

"Owwww!" screamed Walt.

"Boy," said George. "Walt is the dumbest little brother I've ever seen. Come on, Harriet. Let's build a snowman."

"Wowee!" said George. "This is going to be the best snowman ever." And George might have been right . . .

but Walt wrecked it.

"Walt, you are so stupid," said George.
"He was only trying to help," said Harriet.

"Come on," said George. "Let's go sledding. Walt can't wreck that."

So they all climbed the hill. It took Walt a long time.

Harriet and George were already at the bottom again when Walt started down.

"Oh no," said Harriet, "I can't look."

"Boy, what a jerk," said George. "Can't he do anything right?"

"George," said Harriet, "he can't help it. He's just little, that's all."

"He's just dumb," said George.

"Come on, Walt," said Harriet. "Let's go home."

On the way, Harriet taught Walt how to make a snow angel.

And she helped him build a snowman.

And she took him down a hill on her cardboard.

When they got home, it was almost supper time.

"Well," said their mother, "did you have a good time?"

"Once we got rid of George we did," said
Harriet. "Didn't we, Walt?"

But Walt was fast asleep.